Khalida and the Most Beautiful Song

For George Lionheart, who takes care of me.

First published in 2018 by Page Street Kids,
an imprint of
Page Street Publishing Co.
27 Congress Street, Suite 105
Salem, MA 01970
www.pagestreetpublishing.com

Distributed by Macmillan, sales in Canada by The Canadian Manda Group

18 19 20 21 22 CCO 5 4 3 2 1

ISBN-13: 978-1-62414-579-7
ISBN-10: 1-624-14579-5

CIP data for this book is available from the Library of Congress.

This book was typeset in Adorn Bouquet, Lady Love, Livory, and Tuesday Script.
The illustrations were done in graphite, watercolor, and digital.

Printed and bound in China

Page Street Publishing uses only materials from suppliers who are committed to responsible and sustainable forest management.

Page Street Publishing protects our planet by donating to nonprofits like
The Trustees, which focuses on local land conservation.

Khalida and the Most Beautiful Song

Amanda Moeckel

PAGE
STREET
KIDS

Perhaps it was the twinkling of a bright star or the wings of a high-flying owl that awoke the song one night.

It was time.

*K*halida was between barely awake and fast asleep when the song swirled into her bedroom.

It tickled her fingers and dipped into her ear.

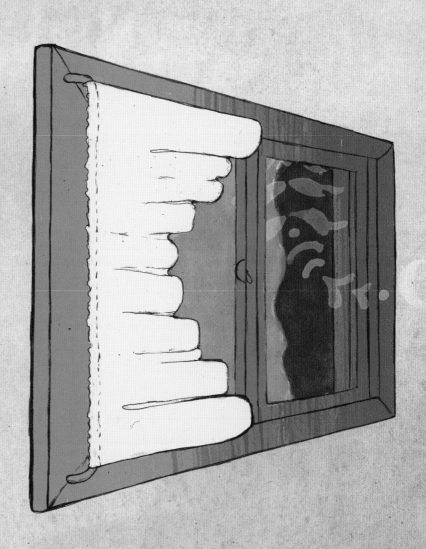

It was a beautiful song.

She had to catch it.

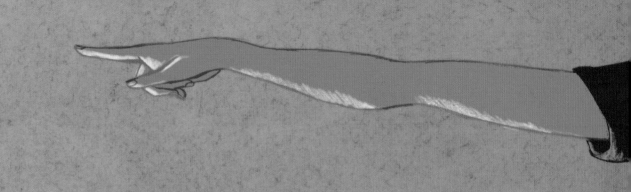

"Back to bed, Khalida! You can play in the morning."

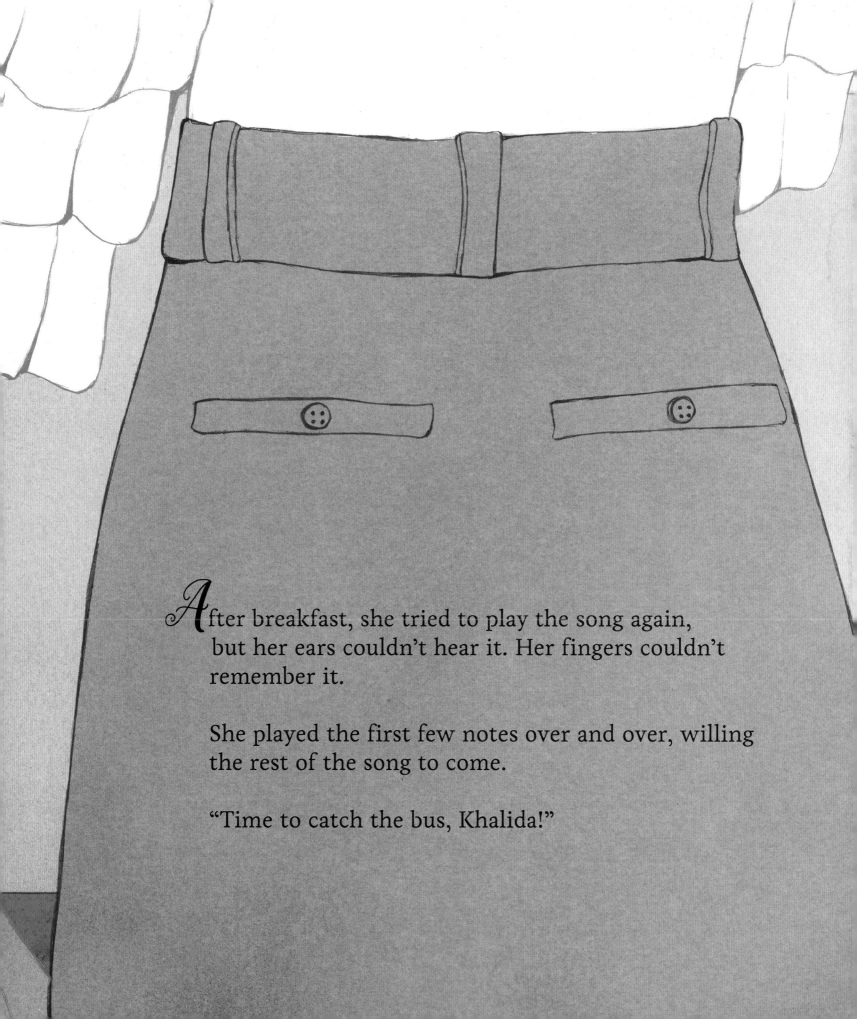

After breakfast, she tried to play the song again, but her ears couldn't hear it. Her fingers couldn't remember it.

She played the first few notes over and over, willing the rest of the song to come.

"Time to catch the bus, Khalida!"

Perhaps it was the butterfly settling on the
windowsill or the sun sending a rainbow
across the chalkboard that made Khalida
hear the song again.

She would catch it this time.

"Back to class, Khalida! Now is not the time."

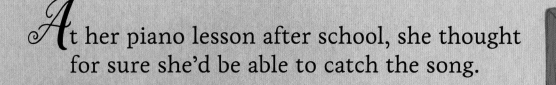

At her piano lesson after school, she thought for sure she'd be able to catch the song.

But once she warmed up and practiced her scales, her head was filled with all the wrong notes.

She plunked away, unable to find the tune.

"Time to go home, Khalida!"

Maybe it was the shimmer of light
on the fountain or the skittering
of pigeons over breadcrumbs,
but pretty soon Khalida heard
the song again.

This time, she had to catch it.

Music flowed through her fingers, onto the keys, and into the air. A crowd gathered . . . and grew.

For a few moments, the people forgot everything else.

Jeremy forgot he was late for a meeting.

Camille forgot about being bullied at school.

Tulip forgot her grandmother was sick.

All they could hear was what Khalida played.

It was the most beautiful song.